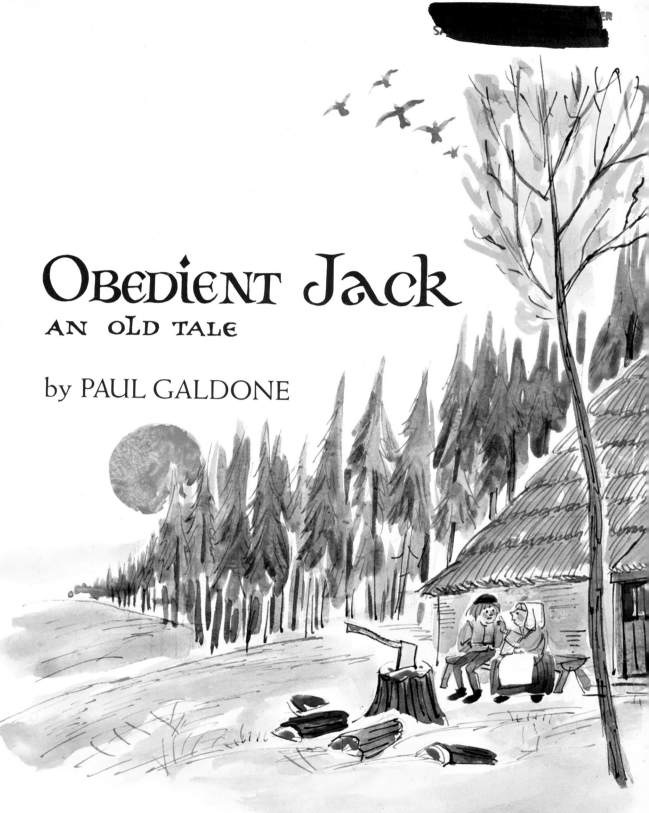

OBEDIENT JACK
AN OLD TALE

by PAUL GALDONE

FRANKLIN WATTS, INC.
845 Third Avenue, New York, N.Y. 10022

For Claudia, Martha
and Granny

SBN 531-01970-5. Library of Congress Catalog Card Number: 72-131155.

Once long ago there was a boy named Jack, who lived with his widowed mother in a small cottage at the edge of the woods.

They were so poor they had hardly enough to eat. As Jack grew older and had a bigger appetite their plight grew worse.

Finally, one day, his mother said to him,
"Jack, it is time you went to work
and earned your own bread."

"Yes, indeed, Mother,
I'll do what you say,"
Jack answered willingly.

The next day, Jack went off
and hired himself to a nearby farmer.

That evening, the farmer paid Jack
a penny for his day's work.

Jack had no pocketbook because
he had never carried money before.
As he walked along, he lost the penny
in the tall weeds beside the road.

"You dunce!" exclaimed his mother
when he arrived home, "you should have put
your earnings in your pocket."

"So sorry, Mother,
I'll do what you say next time."

The following morning, Jack was hired
by a dairyman who paid him with a jug of
milk for his day's work.

Obedient Jack crammed the jug of milk
into his pocket and headed for home.

Of course, all the milk
had splashed out long before
he got there.

"You silly goose,"
scolded his mother,
"you should have carried
it on your head."

"So sorry, Mother,
I'll do what you say
next time."

The next day the dairyman hired Jack again,
and gave him a pound of butter for his pay.
Remembering his mother's advice, Obedient Jack
placed the pound of butter on his head
and pulled his hat over it.

The day was very hot and the butter began to melt.
By the time Jack reached home, his hair, his face,
and his jacket were yellow with melted butter.

"Three days of work, and nothing to show for it,"
cried his mother.

"Don't you know you should have wrapped it in cool
leaves and carried it in your hands?"

"So sorry, Mother, I'll do what
you say next time," promised Jack.

The next day, Obedient Jack found work with
a baker who gave him a big cat in payment.

When he tried to wrap cool leaves around the cat,
it howled and scratched and spat.

Jack could not hold on to it, and had to let it go.

When he got home and his mother heard what had happened, she shouted, "You fool, you simpleton! You should have tied a rope around its neck and led it home."

"So sorry, Mother,
I'll do what you
say next time,"
promised Jack.

The butcher who hired Jack on the following day
paid him with a roast.

Recalling his mother's scolding, Jack tied a rope
around the meat and dragged it behind him.

But soon, hungry dogs gobbled it up.

This time, his mother was really angry.

"Even a blockhead like you," she screamed, "should have known to carry it on your shoulders."

"So sorry, Mother,
I'll do what you say next time,"
promised Jack.

Not discouraged and still cheerful,
Jack hired himself to a stableman
in the nearby town.

At the end of a whole week's work,
Jack's wage was a donkey.

He certainly had something fine
to take home to his mother now!

Remembering his promise
to obey his mother, Jack hoisted
the donkey on his shoulders
and started for home.

The road led past the house of the wealthiest
merchant in town. This merchant was an unhappy
man. He had a beautiful daughter named Joanna,
who could not speak or hear or laugh.

The doctors had told him that if she could be made
to laugh just once, her speech and hearing
would return to her.

So the merchant had proclaimed
all over the countryside that the first man to make
his daughter laugh could have her for his wife.

As Jack trudged along the dusty street he had no idea how funny he looked. The donkey was sprawled on his shoulders, its legs kicking in the air. Suddenly he heard a shout of laughter, then peal after peal of joyful giggles.

Jack looked up at a window in the merchant's fine house. There he saw a girl pointing at him. Then he heard her shout, "Father, come here and see what a sight is to be seen! Ha! Ha! Ho! Ho! Ho! Ho!"

Her father came running.

He saw that his Joanna was laughing
and that her speech and her hearing
were restored to her.

He called down to Jack,
"Set down the donkey and
enter my house.

"You have cured my daughter.
Would you like her for your wife?"

Jack gladly agreed.
The two were married that same day
and lived happily for many years.

Jack's mother, who came to live with them in richness and comfort, had good reason to be glad her son was, indeed,

OBEDIENT JACK.

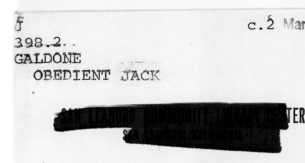